Y0-AFP-404

A catalogue record for this book is available from the British Library

Published by Ladybird Books Ltd
A subsidiary of the Penguin Group
A Pearson Company
LADYBIRD and the device of a Ladybird are trademarks of Ladybird Books Ltd Loughborough Leicestershire UK

Disney's

Beauty and the Beast

Ladybird

Long, long ago, in a far-away castle, there lived a handsome young prince who was very selfish. One stormy night, an old woman carrying a single red rose knocked at his door. "Give me a bed for the night, and I will give you this rose," she said.

The prince looked down at her. "You are much too old and ugly. Just go away," he replied harshly.

"You will be sorry for that," said the old woman, who was really an enchantress. "Now you are going to become a horrible beast. Only if you fall in love with a young girl and she loves you in return will you be saved. But if this rose loses its last petal before that day, you will be a beast for ever!"

There was a little village not far from the castle, where a pretty young girl lived. She was as beautiful as her name – Belle. She was different from other girls of her own age, though. Wherever she went, she had her nose in a book and dreamed of adventure.

"What are you reading today, Belle?" asked the baker.

Belle looked up from her book. "Oh, hello," she said. "It's a wonderful story about a prince who goes through terrible hardships to win his love."

No one in the village really paid much attention when Belle talked of distant countries and princes, although they listened politely.

But there was one person who was annoyed by Belle's books, and that was Gaston. Gaston believed he was much handsomer and stronger than anyone else, and thought Belle should be in love with him.

"That book spoils the view, Belle," he said. "Come for a walk with me instead."

"Leave me in peace!" said Belle crossly. "Now you've made me lose my page. And anyway, I don't want to go for a walk with you."

Belle went back home, where she lived with her father Maurice who was an inventor.

"Come and see, Belle," he said as soon as he saw her. "I've succeeded at last."

Maurice had been inventing machines for years. They usually didn't work and they often exploded.

Belle smiled when she saw her father's latest invention. It was a machine for splitting logs.

"That's really good, Father. You're a genius!" she said warmly.

"I'm going to show it at the fair, Belle. And when I come back, we will be rich!"

It was time for Maurice to go. Belle helped him to harness their horse Philippe, then off he set.

The way led through the forest. But night fell quickly, and soon Maurice was lost.

When he lit his lamp some bats flew straight at him. Then his blood turned to ice. He could see wolves!

Philippe saw them too, and galloped off in a panic. Maurice himself had just one idea left in his head – to escape before the wolves devoured him!

He ran and ran, and suddenly found himself in front of a castle. But when he knocked, there was no answer so he went in.

As soon as Maurice walked through the door, someone said, "Hello, come and warm yourself by the fire. Have you come far?"

Maurice looked round. Who had spoken? Surely it wasn't the candelabra?

"Yes, yes, it's me, Lumiere," said the candelabra. "Mrs Potts the teapot will give you some tea, and Cogsworth the clock will talk to you."

What was all this? A talking candelabra and a teapot called Mrs Potts? And a talking clock as well?

Cogsworth the clock was nervous. He knew their master would be furious. No guests were allowed in the castle.

Maurice sat quietly beside the fire drinking his tea. What a strange place this is, he thought.

Worse was to come. There was a terrifying rumbling noise, then the door burst open. In came an enormous monster. It was the Beast! He was very angry indeed.

"Strangers are not welcome here," he roared. And he carried poor Maurice off to a cold dark dungeon.

Next morning, when Belle got up, the sun was shining brightly in a clear blue sky. She opened the door for some fresh air – and there outside was Philippe!

"Why have you come back alone, Philippe? Where is Father? Something's happened to him!" she cried.

She put on her cloak quickly, then leapt onto Philippe's back. "Come on, Philippe. Take me to where you left him – and hurry."

Belle grew more and more worried as she rode along. Her father must have had an accident, somewhere in this huge forest.

Would she be able to find him? And if he was badly hurt, how could she get him back home?

At last Philippe stopped in front of a big gate. It was now dark, and Belle could only just see the castle in the dimness.

There was something lying on the ground nearby. Belle got down to see what it was.

"It's Father's hat!" she cried, fear in her heart. "Wait here, Philippe. I must go and find out what has happened to him."

Belle hurried into the castle and looked round, but the place seemed empty. She rushed along the gloomy corridors calling, "Father, where are you?"

No one answered. Then Belle found a staircase that led to the dungeons, and she heard a weak groan. It was her father!

He looked back at her through the bars of his cell and said sadly, "Save yourself quickly, Belle. A terrible monster has taken me prisoner."

At that moment the ground began to shake beneath
Belle's feet, and there was a terrible roaring, grunting
noise behind her.

She turned to see the Beast – enormous and very
very ugly.

"My father is old and ill, please let him go," begged
Belle.

"He should not have entered my castle. He deserves to
be punished."

"Please let him go and take me instead."

"If I do that, you must promise to stay for ever."

"Belle, I won't let you do this!" cried Maurice,
horrified.

But Belle promised, and her father was set free.

15

"Since you have promised to stay with me," said the Beast, "this castle is now your home and you can go anywhere you like. All except the west wing, which you must *never* enter."

He showed Belle to her room, then left her.

The moment the door shut behind him, Belle burst into tears. Now she was all alone in this castle, with that horrible Beast.

Then someone spoke. "Come on, it's not that bad. The Beast may be ugly, but he isn't really wicked."

"Who's that?" demanded Belle. "Who spoke?"

"It's me, Wardrobe. You can try all my lovely dresses."

Meanwhile, downstairs, Cogsworth the clock was saying, "If you want the young lady to be interested in you, you must be nice to her. Invite her to dinner!"

"That's a good idea," said the Beast with a smile. He went upstairs and knocked on Belle's door. "Would you care to have dinner with me?" he asked in a gentle voice.

"It's kind of you to ask, but no, thank you," said Belle.

The Beast was furious. "In that case, you won't get anything to eat," he growled.

Belle cried for a long time, then she slept. She woke up in the middle of the night, feeling hungry – *very* hungry indeed.

She opened her bedroom door slowly and looked out. Lumiere and Cogsworth were waiting for her in the corridor.

"Hello," said Belle. "Can you tell me where the kitchen is? I'm sure it's long past dinnertime."

"Of course, Miss. Follow me." And Lumiere lit up the staircase to show her the way.

"We mustn't make a noise," murmured Cogsworth. "If the Beast catches us, we'll be in trouble."

"Oh you!" said Lumiere. "You're afraid of everything…"

Lumiere was full of hope. If only Belle would fall in love with the Beast, the bad spell would be lifted. Everyone would return to their normal selves again, and the castle would be happy once more.

He danced around, encouraging the crockery and the cutlery. "Hurry up, crystal and silver. Come on, cups and teapots. Everyone, there's going to be a feast!"

Lumiere smiled happily as they all got busy, and he went on telling them what to do. "Come on, where are the spoons? Everyone, jump to it! Where's the sugar? And the milk – we mustn't forget the milk!"

Then he turned to Belle. "Here you are, that's a really good cup of tea, Belle. And now, try the rolls."

Everyone had put on a spectacular show for Belle, and she was delighted!

"That was wonderful!" said Belle once the feast was over. "Now, I'd like to look round the castle."

"Of course," said Lumiere. "We'll give you a tour."

But Belle wanted to go by herself. She knew she wasn't allowed in the west wing, but she was terribly curious. Why had the Beast said she wasn't to go there?

She was shocked when she saw it. The Beast's lair was dark and dirty, with cobwebs, cracked mirrors and layers of dust everywhere.

And then, in the very last room, Belle found just one beautiful thing. It was the enchanted rose, glowing inside a glass jar. Belle wanted to see the rose properly, and she lifted the jar.

Suddenly the Beast leapt in through the window. "Get out!" he roared. He took the glass jar from her and put it back over the rose.

"Don't touch this. I told you not to come into the west wing. You don't know the harm you could have done!"

"I'm sorry," said Belle. "I didn't realise it was so serious."

"You have disobeyed me. Get out of my castle," the Beast roared once more.

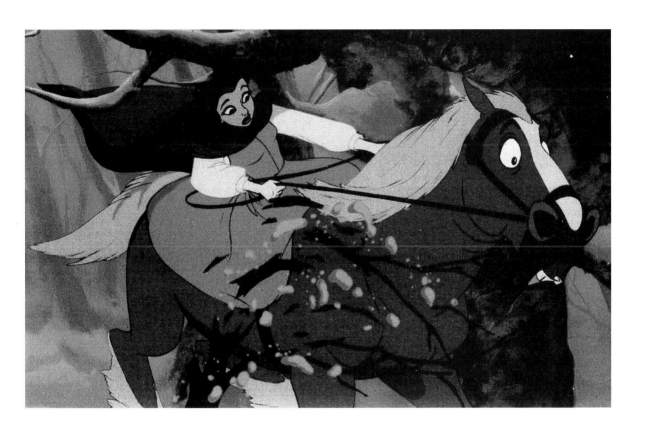

Terrified, Belle didn't need to be told twice. She rushed down the staircase from the west wing and out of the castle as fast as she could. Lumiere and Cogsworth held on to her cloak crying, "Don't leave, Belle, we need you!" but she paid no attention.

Philippe the horse was still waiting where she had left him. As she jumped on his back, Belle heard wolves howling in the distance.

"Quick, Philippe, quick!" cried Belle. But although they set off at full speed through the deep forest, the wolves soon surrounded them. Their yellow eyes gleamed in the darkness. Belle was trapped!

Tired and frightened, Philippe had no strength to fight off a pack of wolves. Belle picked up a big branch and stood in front of him.

The wolves were in no hurry. They knew they had won. They stood round Belle and Philippe in a circle, moving a little closer minute by minute. From time to time they growled, their big teeth shining white in the gloom.

Belle was frightened too. She would have been better off in the castle at the Beast's mercy. At least he only shouted at her!

As the wolves bared their teeth and moved in to attack, Belle tried to defend herself and Philippe.

But it was no good. One of the bigger wolves went straight for her throat.

All at once a huge paw knocked the wolf to one side. The Beast had come to save her!

It was not an easy battle. The Beast was strong and brave, but he was only one against many. He fought hard even when he was badly hurt.

He got rid of the wolves one by one. At last those that were left gave up. They turned tail and disappeared into the forest once more.

The fight was over.

The Beast lay still for a moment, trying to get his strength back. Then Belle helped him to his feet, and they went back to the castle together.

"You have saved my life, Beast, so I will look after you," said Belle. She started to wash his wounds. "Don't worry, you won't feel this much."

"Ouch, you're hurting me," said the Beast.

"It's for your own good," said Belle. "Keep still!"

Surprisingly, when that awful day had at last come to an end, the castle seemed a much happier place. And Belle had lost all fear of the Beast.

They went for a walk together in the gardens of the castle, and Belle told the Beast all about the books she had read. Since Belle was there, the birds even dared to take food from the Beast's large paw.

Inside, everyone was cheerful. "Look at that, Mrs Potts!" said Lumiere. "The Beast is different since Belle came."

"You are quite right," replied his friend. "If only they could fall in love, we could all enjoy life once more. But the Beast is so ugly…"

From that day, Belle began to take all her meals with the Beast, in the great dining room of the castle. Mrs Potts made them lots of delicious things. The Beast gulped his food down, while Belle ate hers daintily.

Belle tried to teach him manners. "You shouldn't make such a noise when you are eating. Try not to drop food on the table. You have beautiful cutlery – learn to use it properly," she would tell him.

"But my paws are so large, and this fork is so small..." pleaded the Beast.

"Just try," said Belle firmly.

But sometimes even Belle would pick up her dish with both hands, just to make the Beast feel at home!

"Belle, why don't we give a ball here, just for the two of us?" the Beast suggested one evening.

"What a good idea, Beast! I'll go and get ready," said Belle, going to her room.

The Beast ran to his room as well. He curled his beard and whiskers, and perfumed himself. But when he looked in the mirror, his heart sank. How silly he looked! Curls weren't for him. So he just washed and changed his clothes. Now, to the ball.

"This evening, my lady, you are even more beautiful than before. If you will take my arm, we will go to the ball together."

"With pleasure, sir," said Belle, smiling.

Everyone who lived in the castle was there, in the great ballroom. Never had the candles burned so brightly, or the music played so delightfully.

Because of Belle, the Beast was happy, and hope was growing in his heart.

He thought of the enchanted rose. It had not yet lost all its petals – was it possible that Belle might one day love him?

"Belle," he asked, "are you happy with me?"

"Yes, Beast," she answered. "You are nice to me, and we are having a good time together. But there's one thing I would like to ask you."

"Ask whatever you wish. I would like you to have everything you want, but I am so frightened I may lose you…" said the poor Beast, looking down at her.

"Well, it's just that I'm worried about my father. I would like to make sure he's all right."

"Belle, here is a magic mirror. In it you will see the person you are thinking of. If you wish to go back to your father, I won't keep you here…"

"Oh, I see him! He's in the forest, not far from here. He looks so old and ill – I'm sure he's searching for me. He needs me so much."

Listening to her, the Beast felt his heart breaking. Belle wanted her father more than him. All was now lost, nothing and no one could help him. But he did not want Belle to be unhappy.

"Belle, you are free to go and find your father. Take the mirror and think of me sometimes…"

"Oh, thank you, Beast. You are so kind!"

Within a very short time, Belle was on her way. Thanks to the magic mirror, she soon found her father in the depths of the forest.

He was so weak that she almost had to carry him.

"Everything will be all right now, Father," she said.

"But the Beast – how did you escape?" he asked.

"I didn't have to escape, he let me go. I'm not frightened of him now, I like him," Belle told him. "He has changed. He is always kind and gentle now."

In the village, they could talk of nothing but Belle's return. Gaston was more upset than anyone. The Beast had held Belle prisoner – and she was the girl Gaston wanted to marry. He made up his mind to rid the world of this monster.

"Come on," he said to his friends. "Let's go and ask Belle to lead us to the Beast's castle."

When Belle opened the door and heard what they wanted, she was angry. "You don't know what you're talking about. The Beast may be ugly, but he isn't wicked. He is very kind. Look in this magic mirror and see for yourselves…"

When the crowd saw the Beast in the mirror, they were terrified.

But Gaston yelled, "Don't listen to her. "Belle, give me that mirror. We will go and kill the Beast, and afterwards, you will marry me." Belle's words had made him mad with jealousy. Belle tried to stop him but he wouldn't listen.

The villagers armed themselves with guns and thick sticks and waited.

"Forward! Forward!" Gaston cried. "As long as this terrible Beast lives, no young girl will be safe. It is for us, all of us here, to rid the world of such a dangerous creature. Let us go in force to the castle, and kill the Beast before he kills us!"

With these stirring words, Gaston led his men into the forest. They marched close together, looking round fearfully.

Soon they were at the castle, but the door was closed against them. So they broke it down.

Inside the great hall of the castle, the villagers stopped and stared. They had never seen such magnificence.

Gaston wasn't so impressed. He ran from room to room calling, "Where are you, Beast? Show yourself and fight!" But all was silent.

The Beast was growing weaker and weaker. He lay at the top of a tower, watching for Belle. When Gaston found him, he paid no attention to him at all.

Suddenly, without warning, the Beast stood up. Belle and her father had just arrived. He felt all his strength flooding back.

He caught hold of Gaston and dangled him over the side of the tower.

"No, no, stop!" cried Belle, taking the stairs two at a time.

The Beast heard Belle's voice and paused. "You don't deserve to live, but I will spare your life, because I love Belle."

These words made Gaston even more angry. But he could tell that the Beast was much, much stronger than him…

The Beast bounded towards the balcony where Belle was waiting, and they ran into each other's arms.

Gaston had hidden nearby. When he saw them together, he was so jealous that he threw himself on the Beast and stabbed him.

With a cry of pain, the Beast swung round and tore his dagger from him.

Gaston backed away, shouting, "Help! Help!"

The Beast's eyes never left Belle's as he slowly sank to the ground, wounded. He groaned weakly.

Belle knelt beside him, tears rolling down her cheeks. "I'm here, I've come back. Everything's going to be all right now." But the Beast just groaned. "It's me, Belle. It's all my fault, I should never have left you. Please don't die, Beast, I need you!"

"At least I've seen you one more time," gasped the Beast. "But it's too late. The last petal is falling from the rose. Perhaps it's better like this…"

"No, no, don't leave me," cried Belle. "I love you!"

The Beast's eyes closed. He lay still. Belle lay by his side, sobbing her heart out.

Then something strange happened. The Beast's body seemed to melt into thin air and disappear.

Belle looked up to see a handsome young man standing in front of her. He looked at her tenderly, and bent down to kiss her.

"Belle, it's me, your Beast. Your love has broken the spell that has held me all these years."

In the west wing, the enchanted rose was alive once more. The mist that had hung over the castle for so long floated away, and the sun shone bright in a clear blue sky.

The castle itself was full of life and light. Cogsworth, Mrs Potts and Lumiere were again the cheerful, friendly servants they had been before the spell had changed them.

Lumiere's face was the picture of happiness. "Long live Belle and the prince!" he cried.

A ball was held at the castle to celebrate everyone's new-found happiness.

The prince looked down at Belle as they danced. "Belle," he said, "I could only be saved by someone who loved me, and the Beast is no more. Will you marry me?"

"Dear prince, I loved the Beast with his big teeth and gruff voice. Now you are gentle and handsome, and I still love you – and for ever and ever."